HISTORY'S KID
HEROES

# THE PRISON-SHIP ADVENTURE OF JAMES FORTEN,

# REVOLUTIONARY WAR CAPTIVE

BY **MARTY RHODES FIGLEY**
ADAPTATION BY **AMANDA DOERING TOURVILLE**
ILLUSTRATED BY **TED HAMMOND** AND **RICHARD PIMENTEL CARBAJAL**

Graphic Universe™ Minneapolis • New York

# INTRODUCTION

JAMES FORTEN WAS BORN ON SEPTEMBER 2, 1766, IN PHILADELPHIA, PENNSYLVANIA. PHILADELPHIA WAS THE LARGEST CITY IN THE AMERICAN COLONIES. JAMES'S PARENTS WERE FREE AFRICAN AMERICANS, BUT HIS GRANDPARENTS HAD BEEN SLAVES.

JAMES'S FATHER WAS A SAILMAKER. AS A YOUNG BOY, JAMES WENT TO WORK WITH HIS FATHER, LEARNING TO MAKE SAILS. WHEN JAMES WAS SEVEN YEARS OLD, HIS FATHER DIED. FOR A FEW YEARS, JAMES WENT TO A QUAKER SCHOOL. HE LEARNED TO READ AND TO WORK WITH NUMBERS. BUT HIS FAMILY NEEDED MONEY, SO JAMES TOOK A JOB IN A STORE. JAMES GAVE THE MONEY HE EARNED TO HIS FAMILY.

AT THIS TIME, GREAT BRITAIN RULED THE COLONIES. BUT BY THE 1770S, THE COLONISTS WANTED THEIR FREEDOM. IN 1776, THE LEADERS OF THE

AMERICAN COLONIES SIGNED THE DECLARATION OF INDEPENDENCE. THIS
DOCUMENT SAID THAT AMERICA WAS A NEW COUNTRY FREE FROM GREAT
BRITAIN. JAMES JOINED THE CROWD IN PHILADELPHIA TO HEAR THE
DECLARATION READ TO THE PUBLIC FOR THE FIRST TIME. BUT AMERICA
WOULD STILL HAVE TO FIGHT GREAT BRITAIN FOR ITS INDEPENDENCE.

JAMES WANTED TO DO HIS PART TO HELP AMERICA
WIN ITS FREEDOM. HE WENT TO SEA ON THE *ROYAL
LOUIS*, A PRIVATELY OWNED SHIP THAT HELPED
THE AMERICAN CAUSE. HIS JOB WAS TO BRING
GUNPOWDER TO THE SHIP'S CANNONS. HIS DESIRE
TO HELP WAS ABOUT TO BE TESTED.

BOOM!

ALL HANDS ON DECK, MEN!

6

JAMES AND HENRY BECAME FRIENDS. THEY PLAYED MARBLES AND EXPLORED THE SHIP TOGETHER.

BUT JAMES KNEW THIS FREEDOM WOULDN'T LAST.

THE AMPHION WAS SAILING TOWARD NEW YORK HARBOR. THERE, THE REST OF THE PRISONERS, INCLUDING JAMES, WOULD BE TAKEN TO THE PRISON SHIP JERSEY.

# AFTERWORD

AFTER JAMES LEFT THE *AMPHION*, HE NEVER SAW CAPTAIN BAZELY OR HENRY AGAIN. JAMES LATER SPOKE ABOUT HIS EXPERIENCE: "THUS . . . DID A GAME OF MARBLES SAVE [ME] FROM A LIFE OF . . . SERVITUDE."

FELLOW PRISONER DANIEL BREWTON SURVIVED. HE NEVER FORGOT JAMES FORTEN'S KINDNESS IN HELPING HIM ESCAPE FROM THE *JERSEY*. DANIEL KNEW THAT JAMES HAD SAVED HIS LIFE. THE TWO MEN BECAME LIFELONG FRIENDS.

AFTER THE WAR, JAMES FORTEN EVENTUALLY RETURNED TO THE SAILMAKING SHOP WHERE HIS FATHER HAD WORKED. BY THE AGE OF 32, JAMES OWNED THE SHOP. HE EMPLOYED 40 MEN, BOTH WHITE AND BLACK. HE BECAME ONE OF THE WEALTHIEST MEN IN PHILADELPHIA.

JAMES BELIEVED THAT ALL BLACK AMERICANS WERE ENTITLED TO THE SAME RIGHTS ENJOYED BY WHITE CITIZENS. HE WAS ACTIVE IN THE ANTISLAVERY MOVEMENT AND HELPED FUND THE FAMOUS ABOLITIONIST NEWSPAPER THE *LIBERATOR*. JAMES FORTEN DIED ON MARCH 4, 1842. MORE THAN 3,000 PEOPLE, BOTH BLACK AND WHITE, ATTENDED HIS FUNERAL.

# FURTHER READING AND WEBSITES

ALPHIN, ELAINE MARIE, AND ARTHUR B. ALPHIN. *I HAVE NOT YET BEGUN TO FIGHT: A STORY ABOUT JOHN PAUL JONES.* MINNEAPOLIS: MILLBROOK PRESS, 2004.

AMERICA'S STORY FROM AMERICA'S LIBRARY: REVOLUTIONARY PERIOD HTTP://WWW.AMERICASLIBRARY.GOV/JB/REVOLUT/JB_REVOLUT_SUBJ .HTML

AMSTEL, MARSHA. *THE HORSE-RIDING ADVENTURE OF SYBIL LUDINGTON, REVOLUTIONARY WAR MESSENGER.* MINNEAPOLIS: GRAPHIC UNIVERSE, 2011.

FIGLEY, MARTY RHODES. *JOHN GREENWOOD'S JOURNEY TO BUNKER HILL.* MINNEAPOLIS: MILLBROOK PRESS, 2011.

HASKINS, JIM. *BLACK STARS OF COLONIAL TIMES AND THE REVOLUTIONARY WAR: AFRICAN AMERICANS WHO LIVED THEIR DREAMS.* NEW YORK: JOSSEY-BASS, 2002.

HAUGEN, DAVID, ED. *VOICES OF THE REVOLUTIONARY WAR: SOLDIERS.* SAN DIEGO: BLACKBIRCH PRESS, 2004.

HISTORICAL MARKERS. EXPLORE PENNSYLVANIA HISTORY HTTP://EXPLOREPAHISTORY.COM/HMARKER.PHP?MARKERID=870

JAMES FORTEN. BLACK INVENTOR ONLINE MUSEUM HTTP://WWW.BLACKINVENTOR.COM/PAGES/JAMES-FORTEN.HTML

KREBS, LAURIE. *A DAY IN THE LIFE OF A COLONIAL SAILMAKER.* NEW YORK: POWERKIDS PRESS, 2004.

MILLER, BRANDON MARIE. *GROWING UP IN REVOLUTION AND THE NEW NATION 1775–1800.* MINNEAPOLIS: LERNER PUBLICATIONS COMPANY, 2003.

ROOP, PETER, AND CONNIE ROOP. *THE TOP-SECRET ADVENTURE OF JOHN DARRAGH, REVOLUTIONARY WAR SPY.* MINNEAPOLIS: GRAPHIC UNIVERSE, 2011.

## ABOUT THE AUTHOR

MARTY RHODES FIGLEY LIVES IN ANNANDALE, VIRGINIA, WITH HER HUSBAND AND AIREDALE TERRIER, SCARLETT. SHE ENJOYS PLAYING THE ROLE OF "HISTORY DETECTIVE" AS SHE DOES THE RESEARCH FOR HER HISTORICALLY BASED CHILDREN'S BOOKS. MARTY LOVES TO DELVE INTO OLD BOOKS, LETTERS, AND NEWSPAPERS; VISIT MUSEUMS; AND EXPLORE FAMOUS HISTORICAL SITES.

## ABOUT THE ADAPTER

AMANDA DOERING TOURVILLE HAS WRITTEN MORE THAN 40 BOOKS FOR CHILDREN. TOURVILLE IS GREATLY HONORED TO WRITE FOR YOUNG PEOPLE AND HOPES THAT THEY WILL LEARN TO LOVE READING AND LEARNING AS MUCH AS SHE DOES. WHEN NOT WRITING, TOURVILLE ENJOYS TRAVELING, PHOTOGRAPHY, AND HIKING. SHE LIVES IN MINNESOTA WITH HER HUSBAND AND GUINEA PIG.

## ABOUT THE ILLUSTRATORS

TED HAMMOND IS A CANADIAN ARTIST, LIVING AND WORKING JUST OUTSIDE OF TORONTO. HAMMOND HAS CREATED ARTWORK FOR EVERYTHING FROM FANTASY AND COMIC-BOOK ART TO CHILDREN'S MAGAZINES, POSTERS, AND BOOK ILLUSTRATION.

RICHARD CARBAJAL HAS A BROAD SPECTRUM OF ILLUSTRATIVE SPECIALTIES. HIS BACKGROUND HAS FOCUSED ON LARGE-SCALE INSTALLATIONS AND SCENERY. CARBAJAL RECENTLY HAS EXPANDED INTO THE BOOK PUBLISHING AND ADVERTISING MARKETS.

Text copyright © 2011 by Lerner Publishing Group, Inc.
Illustrations © 2011 by Lerner Publishing Group, Inc.

Graphic Universe™ is a trademark of Lerner Publishing Group, Inc.

All rights reserved. International copyright secured. No part of this book may be reproduced, stored in a retrieval system, or transmitted in any form or by any means—electronic, mechanical, photocopying, recording, or otherwise—without the prior written permission of Lerner Publishing Group, Inc., except for the inclusion of brief quotations in an acknowledged review.

Graphic Universe™
A division of Lerner Publishing Group, Inc.
241 First Avenue North
Minneapolis, MN 55401 U.S.A.

Website address: www.lernerbooks.com

Figley, Marty Rhodes, 1948–
    The prison-ship adventure of James Forten, Revolutionary War captive / by Marty Rhodes Figley; adapted by Amanda Doering Tourville; illustrated by Ted Hammond and Richard Carbajal.
    p.   cm. — (History's kid heroes)
    Summary: In 1781, fifteen-year-old James Forten, a free African American from Philadelphia, is proud to be fighting for the American colonies, but when the British capture the ship on which he serves he fears for both his life and his freedom.
    Includes bibliographical references.
    ISBN: 978–0–7613–6183–1 (lib. bdg. : alk. paper)  1. Forten, James, 1766–1842—Juvenile fiction.  2. Graphic novels.
[1. Graphic novels.  2. Forten, James, 1766–1842—Fiction.  3. African Americans—Fiction.  4. Prisoners—Fiction.
5. United States—History—Revolution, 1775–1783—Fiction.]  I. Tourville, Amanda Doering.  II. Hammond, Ted, ill.
III. Carbajal, Richard, ill.  IV. Title.
PZ7.7.T68Pri 2011
973.3'71—dc22                                                                                              2010035204

Manufactured in the United States of America
1—CG—12/31/10